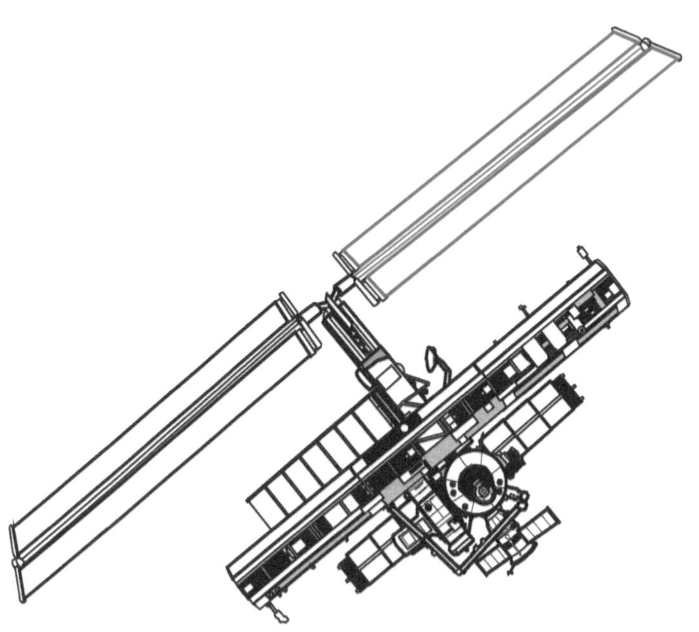

DEEP OVERSTOCK

#1: Space Exploration

May 2018

“ Space is the breath of art. 

Frank Lloyd Wright

ASTRO - SPACE EXPLORATION

Letter from the Editors

Dear Readers,

Thank you for picking up the first issue of Deep Overstock, the booksellers' journal.

We started Deep Overstock to get booksellers connected and working together. Powell's is what, 80% writers, illustrators and comics artists? 90%? We wanted a deadline and a venue. Our dream is to host international bookseller barbecues--hmu if you're down. We read and read and read and read. (For some/most of us to avoid the death spiral of our own inner-mind. (inner-mind? (inner space!))) Working at a bookstore, you get to know and love many genres.

We theme each issue because we want to dive into genre, whether it be space exploration, dark fantasy, self help, fairy tales, metaphysics or paranormal romance. Our editorial board works at Powell's so we are constantly surrounded by a million books on every subject. There is no kind of book we haven't shelved (even sexy books and books on mushroom diseases!).

We take the theme of our journal from one category of books and interpret the category as we see fit. For our inaugural issue we chose Space Exploration. Although "space exploration" falls under Astronomy, space can be interpreted in any number of ways (personal space, interpersonal space, physical space).

Submitters then had one month to submit pieces of their interpretation of the theme. We welcome any sort of creative endeavor be it poem, short story, very short story, drawing, comic, recipe, play, interpretive dance, song, etc.

We're looking forward to our next issue: Fairy Tales, Folktales, and Fables. If you're reading this submissions are open, and will close June 1st. Spin us a yarn!

Signed,

Deep Overstock's Editors

On the Shelves

Kyrithka

by Jonathan van Belle

Planet 7Y7H is an undead world.

The native human-like species called themselves "Ijj"--origin and meaning unknown. And they called their planet, "Ijjadyn".

History: Thousands of years ago on Ijjadyn, in the period known as "Thrithu-Jish" ["Thrithu-Jish", transl. "After the Fall of Jish"; "Jish" unknown], a period we have classified as Ijjadyn's Late-Modern Period, there occurred a global religious movement: The "Mizru".

"Mizru" comes from the name "Yof-Yyzu-Mizru"--the name of a murky, mostly unknown Messianic figure from the northern pole regions of Ijjadyn, in an area called "Ugarim, Skyll um-Aphyki" (Ugarim, the High Dominion of Aph the "Ice-Reader").

[Note: the word "yki" means roughly "Ice-reader". Naturally, an ice-reader is one who "reads" the ice. Ice-reading is "divination by ice," or what is sometimes called "glaciemancy". Ice-reading usually took the form of an examination of snow-crystal formations under a magnifying lens, a device called the "Ottyki"-- the "Eye of the Ice-Reader"]

What we know of Yof-Yyzu-Mizru: First, everything we know of Yof-Yyzu-Mizru comes from a set of records, called "Yyki-Yyzu-Mizru" left by Mizru clerics. "Yyki" is a variation of "yki", and means "ice-readings"; thus the record's title translates almost literally as: "The Ice-Readings of Yyzu-Mizru".

From the Ice-Readings, we find out the following: Mizru was an Ugarim male living in the period known as Gythu-Jish ["Before the Fall of Jish"]--what we classify as Ijjadyn's Early-Modern Period.

In Mizru's early life, at the Ijjadyn age of Daza-Ek [which means "12", but is something like 11-13 Earth years], he became "Zyyluzim" [Zyy-"God" + luzim-"Frozen" = "God-Frozen"], which seems to mean that Yof-Yyzu-Mizru suffered some serious form of paralysis [Compare the word "luzim" with the Thrithu-Jish-Ugarim word, a.k.a. Late Modern Ugarim word, "Lyzmim"--meaning: "paralysis"].

The Ugarim word "Zyy" [God] has origins, we now believe, in the very ancient Ugarim word "Zyv", which translates as "abysses in abysses". Ironically, it seems that primitive Ijj were atheistic. The existence of a non-sentient, non-Ijj-like, and non-personal Zyv was a profound thing to primitive Ijj, so much so that it slowly evolved, in the Early-Modern Period, into something sentient, Ijj-like, and personal: Zyy. I say that this is ironic, and I mean this in comparison with our own human development. Ijjadyn represents something like the theological reverse of Earth: Ijjadyn trended from global non-theism to global theism.

In Early-Modern Ugarim mythology, and later in Late-Modern Ijjadyn mythology, the Zyyluzim were considered to be oracular; the Zyyluzim were "frozen" divine messengers for Zyy. In the Ice-Readings, we hear of earlier Zyyluzim, those before Mizru. For example, we hear of the Zyyluzim-Yar-Hyf-Izin, who predicted the arrival of "Zyyluzim um-Skyllu um-Skyllu" or "A God-Frozen [oracle] of the Highest Dominion of the Highest Dominion". Believers in Mizru argued that this prediction referred to Yof-Yyzu-Mizru.

The Late-Modern Mizru movement, among many other things, accepted a tenet called "Yzryotti"or "Open Eyes", found in the final section of the Ice-Readings--a section called "Yyullu"-- "Death".

The tenet of Yzryotti is derived from Yyullu Diza-Uk ["Death Number 27"], which reads, in English, as follows: "Ijjix [infant Ijj], if they die upon the first opening of their eyes, go directly to Yythga [Heaven]. From them is a vast river of hyrk [sinless] Atmithi [souls] that flows unimpeded to Yarvadyn [Alternate name for Heaven, meaning something like "Paradise"]."

[Note: This "vast river of sinless souls", first used metaphorically, later became literal, and was known as "Hyrkukra" (roughly "sinless river" or "sinless rapids")]

This movement, therefore, invented "Kyrithka" (which, loosely, means "Heaven-Flowering"). Kyrithka is a Type VII machine, but non-human. Type VII machines are self-cleaning, self-repairing, and generally self-sustaining. While not classifiably A.I., Kyrithka is indicated to be a PIM-Learning exo-machine, and was constructed with defensive or self-preserving weaponry of an as yet unstudied kind.

Kyrithka is, in brief, millenia-proof.

Kyrithka is capable of artificially producing Ijjix; parents are not required. Kyrithka then terminates each cycle of its Ijjix production, precisely at the moments their eyes open.

After producing Kyrithka, the Mizru initiated two radical actions: mass homicide and mass suicide. The Mizru killed the non-Mizru of Ijjadyn, calling this action: "Hylrithka"--or, Hell-Flowering. This was soon followed by the mass suicide of the Mizru, the "Nilrithka".

Upon the total extinction of non-Mizru (an extinction thoroughly confirmed by the Mizru, given their meticulous and advanced systems of cognitive codification), the Mizru initiated "Nilrithka" -- or, "No-Flowering" (Their "nil-" being improbably similar to our Latin "nil", meaning "nothing"). Nilrithka was a mass suicide. This radical event was called Nilrithka, or No-Flowering, because, according to the Ice-Readings of Mizru, suicide obliterates the "Atmith" [translated into something like; "Above-This"], an entity which is comparable to the "soul" in some of our earth mythologies.

Thus, the Mizru believed that Nilrithka meant the extinction of their own Atmithi (the plural form of Atmith). Why, then, commit Nilrithka? This remains unclear.

Once Nilrithka was complete, and all the Ijj on Ijjadyn were dead, the mindless machine Kyrithka began operating, using its organic store to begin its endless reproductive cycles. And now, some untold number of millennia later, Kyrithka still runs. For all this time, this mindless machine has been producing and executing fields of infant Ijj. Isolated on 7Y7H, Kyrithka births and kills. This ice-webbed and Earth-sized planet is a headless, mindless, growing grave.

-- Excerpt from *An Overview of Late-Modern Ijjadyn and the Birth of Kyrithka* by Klima Jostenson, Exosociologist from U.V.V. [Decembra 11, 2507 (E).]

Andy Rides the MAX again

by Andy Anderson

I took a ride on the MAX to SE, Orange line to Milwaukee, post full moon chaos, it was a new day

A little sun burnt from nude beach on Tuesday and a little sore from cannabis infused yoga on Wednesday

Now it's Friday

"No, I won't be going out this weekend," Andy said, "maybe next weekend."

Today a beer at Tugboat with Juliet Palante, the main character in a Gabby Rivera novel

I'm dying to become a reliable something on the page too, to become something. Anything.

Then more time on the MAX

There was a what? A murder? A stabbing?

On the MAX today

At Hollywood Station

I know that stop well

Three throats slit for standing up for two girls, brown, one wearing a hijab

This is what they are saying What are they saying?

There is a bike hanging on a Not-In-Service train I see it pass as I wait again to go home

Who left it?

Are they even alive? All I feel is darkness

It's all that's left

Andy rides the MAX home, it's late. They have a repulsion/attraction to fear.

Sensitive, but Solid. Astrologically, fearless.

They ride and make hard sketch lines in their journal until the page turns black and simultaneously write a poem titled An Ode To My Etch A Sketch.

An Ode To My Etch A Sketch

by Andy Anderson

I etch

And etch

And etch In the same square

Until I can see the insides

My insides

Through it

Fine repeating strokes over

And over

Side by side I transform the medium

And myself in it

Displacing aluminum powder

Until every speck squeaks away

Scraping and scraping

Drawing over the same lines to erase

No longer a canvas

Instead a window

The workings no longer a secret

Can you see?

Look inside

No more surface

Hours of pencil free drawing Look what I etched

I erased the entire thing I created something else

On the Sky in South Texas

by Joe Galván

If you grew up in a neighborhood like mine—a neighborhood with broken concrete sidewalks and huge tropical trees—summer afternoons were spent outside, under the carport of your house, if you were lucky to have one. It didn't matter if the weather had been sufficiently pleasant (it was never pleasant in the early evenings, unless it had just rained, or was about to). We didn't have cable so my mother would make cold cut sandwiches for my grandfather, while my grandfather would carry out the largest TV we had in the house—an old Signature 2000 from Montgomery Ward, before it went under—and swatting away the mosquitoes and the horseflies, sweltering under the carport's oppressive ninety-degree heat, my grandfather would watch Diagnosis Murder with Dick Van Dyke. The year this happened was either 1994 or 1995. I was ten or eleven years old. I don't know how people could pay attention to shows like that, but we did. After dinner we'd have huge scoops of pecan praline ice cream and talk in-between the commercials. The glare from the blue sky washed out the TV's reception and our TV still had dials. You had to use a pair of rubber pliers to change the channel and risk electrocuting yourself in the process.

In South Texas there are three realities: the sky and the sun, and their effects on everything.

After the sun set, though, the fluorescent light under the carport would come on and my grandfather would settle in to have his last cigar of the evening. I'd walk out into the backyard, away from the glare of the fluorescent light and the TV. If there was a cool wind blowing, I would have felt it shudder the tender leaves of the chinaberry tree. Through that tree I could see the first stars in the deep hues of twilight, at first distant and silvery, then suddenly present in all their different hues and colors. The opening in-between the two chinaberry trees in the backyard framed the constellations of Libra, Scorpius and Sagittarius perfectly—in the purple and blue haze of civil twilight one could ascertain the thin and wispy fronds of millions of light-years of cosmic gases and dust, the cradle of stars and planets, the heart of the Universe. Indeed, early on, I learned that this region of the sky was like looking through a crystal ball and seeing beyond the eons of earthly time, back to the beginning of the Big Bang.

The sky had become like an open canvas. It was during the many years of my young life, the only real friend I had. Pacing back and forth on the warm strip of concrete that linked my house with my aunt's, I would read Madame Bovary out loud under a blue sky flecked with puffy white clouds that turned pink and violet as the sunset, then a powdery blue, and imagined I was Emma Bovary, experiencing the illicit and the profane in the Norman countryside of the 1840s, and there I was, profoundly alone and neglected reading that book to myself, over the sound of the din of America's Most Wanted playing from a TV just outside my mother's window. In the spring—the best nights to stargaze in South Texas—I could see Hydra and Virgo and Leo through a pair of cheap binoculars borrowed from my uncle, and would spy through them the immense but dim Virgo clusters, sisters of the Milky Way, spinning into oblivion. The sky was still dark in a town like mine, cut off from the rest of America and sitting there at the edge of the world like a dark little ember. The summers were full of heat lightning and dust. There was no wind except for those nights when a tropical storm made landfall. The lightning would start in the west, a series of brilliant white and blue flashes in the middle of the night, premonitory and mysterious, and the thunder that came through the eaves of the house with it was round and blue and full as it moved through toward the ground. But in the morning, the ground was wet and everything was suddenly lush and green and cool. I could hear my aunt singing alabanzas to the Sacred Heart as she dumped out the collected rainwater onto her gardenias.

From the carport of my house I could see the round moon on certain nights, big as a half-dollar piece, arise like a fat yellow round above the ocean and float like a bubble through the pata de vaca and my aunt's crêpe myrtles. Once, on a fine August evening, I pointed out the moon to my grandfather and his pants fell down, and we all had a laugh. That night had been cool because it had rained that afternoon and the ground was still cool and wet. The moon then became round and silvery and distant. It hung as low in the sky as the sun did in winter, casting romantic shadows against the white houses in the middle of the night, as I snuck out of my house to observe the midnight blue and the light of the moon alighting on a thunderhead in the north.

Most of the time, though, the sky was big and dark and empty. Into it went everything different I wished about my life. I had seen other skies (in West Texas, in New Mexico, and in Brazil), but nothing that empty or that lonely had existed anywhere else. It was only on those clear, settled evenings in the late spring that the world seemed possible; that the stars themselves were close enough to reach out and touch, that I was not as inferior or as damaged as I thought I was.

One day, long after all of my troubles were through, I imagined I floated up and away just as the sun was setting, passing like smoke through the trees and past the lilac flowers of the chinaberry or even the immense pecan trees. That was how all the dreams I had seemed to start—I would just ascend and fade into the forgotten blue of a twilit sky, my eyes closing and opening among the stars, my eyes fixed on the perfect sapphire of those skies which no longer exist.

ALIEN

by Geoff Wallace & Chad Hardy

xx
I want to stare at you, lock tractor beams.
Drinking coffee. Leaning back occasionally.
Staring at the control panels
buried in the other.

I want some kind of ship with a little
incentive, the headless body
of a hard work – a small locker
containing movement, a slot
on the trigger. I don't realize what it is
that worries me.

If I say I'm sick of men –
splatter me with fluids and food
and metal removed from the ground
to kill hysteria – this damn
electrical fire in my body
Keeps overloading
what was semi-transparent –

that I'm sick of their contents

these seven gowns
hanging motionless

like puffing, groggy surgical gloves.

xx
Distressed ivory shines in your body
Tears away at the spongy surface –

The door looking for a ram –
the apertures that spill out what they see
based on nutritional requirements.

And the door blows open.
And the cat moans.

xx
I should be all you ever sleep with – a robot
screwed on a metal deck, programmed
to haul cargo for you.

Stares / Hefts / Touches / Peels

Bring me that light speed
and an incubator – I'm starving
Woven through the jammed
round opening at your cheek

my decision was to be completely healed over
Huddled under the sound
of rending metal

which only appears to be a whole system.

xx
I enter the individual
how divers ascending toward a new reading
penetrate only what hurts.

I'm searching for a smear
of human life
hanging from the landscape

The blood on your
hands and chest

The back of your mouth
The back of your mouth nearby lattice

is quiet

Beneath the oily window.

xx
Time is a molten blast. Another. Another blast.
Another lid that pops open. Row after row.

Turns out the transmission is inside that
flamethrower over there

sitting up

It Leans / Shines / Shines / Snaps / Rigs / Begins
then suddenly makes a loud groaning noise

and the science is all wet.

I want to work but can't.

XX
The cat hovers over my machine
illuminating the grooves.

bizarre extrusions on plexiglass appendages
the future fossilized in distance.

another combination of nothing new

an opaque surface that wrenches
that comes loose in bed
200,000,000 tons of fine, white
silk-like material

You could get cramps staring into the stain.

And here you come up against
a featureless ground
the night-shrouded torso
the source of breath

I labor just to slip
in the wake of you

to fall into the appropriate switches
swallowing sleep
like some kind of table you admire.

xx
your mind bank is a leathery thing
with a complicated biology
able to touch the bridge
to have been ripped.

It levitates.

xx
Below us, night's tide rolls
across the X-ray, smoldering
fragments with a little
creature in reverse position

listening on the frontier
listening a long moment –

it's still like some horrible dream
about dealing with a primitive image of order

about running with instruments into a huge cocoon.

Exhaustion of a Limbo

by Jake Ayres

Each place continues to yield its own quiddities, its own miraculous movements, and its own tragedies.

- C.D. Wright

What a strange place to wake
up in — some beachy thing
str e tched taut across the earth
thin as balloon – skin. Sniff sniff :
Salt. Dimethyl sulfide. You know,
that ocean smell. Invisible krill –
clouds wafting around (really
invisible? (may as well be)). A whale
dips through the sky — slow breach
below the surface layer dark
milk – cloud cover for air.
Me too, big guy, I'm here
breathing like you : we're
taking our time, been here before,
holding it in,
swallowing tiny things that give
themselves away so easily ;
myopic 'til it matters
what's just out of reach —.

Whale – friend rises out of sight,
back to the pod, perhaps, or that
lonely blue above the neutral
gray – blanket – ceiling ;
some seagulls eye my fries,
rats with wings my dad
used to say, my brother
always the one to toss them
a few, as if that makes
a difference ; the swarm comes
regardless who beckons.

The gulls dance and sing
like they just learned to fly.
What is that certain shine,
the sheen of feathers in wind : I
Remember now I wasn't taught to walk,
not really, nor to sleep, I just
sort of found them there
waiting for their host   to arrive.
Licking the ketchup off a finger   I wonder
about all the ways to be lost.
The gulls give up on me.

I miss my whale – friend.
Things were simpler with you
dipping up and down, giant
ovioid eye eye-ing my life :
I'd never felt so beheld.
Mom's shadow   back there
on the boardwalk : growing taller
all the time ;
she cools my forehead even
turned around.

I sense the sand   creeping over
my towel now,   stretching
for my wallet   my phone my
keys—   *how will you leave*
this place without them
the octopus asks, camouflaged
to the nines like a shovel
and pail, you cannot exist
without things !   things !   things !
kept close to your body
you must live like
the cephalopod, we've got it
all figured out,   I can squeeze
through just about anything
see   and octopus buttons itself up and slips
through a crack in a sandcastle—

I don't know how
to respond to a cephalopod
so I bury myself up

to my neck and wait
for the tide to come in
and it does (flash flood)
so now I'm under the sea :
I see every friend I've ever
lost touch with waving slowly—
I start to wave back, but then
whale - friend pokes its head
beneath the water and smiles
that big beautiful cetacean - smile,
sings, *hey man*
we're all here
we're all buried
we're all working on it
well—

wow
look at the size of that krill - cloud
see you later!

—tide goes out—

there are too many things
too many things
to think about I hear an albatross say
as it carves through the air
back to its nest on an impossible cliff.
The sun hasn't budged an inch.
On the warm sand my body
nestles under soft, fine time,
sure heat tip - toes into my eyes
and knowingly nudges me again into absence.

End of Space Exploration

by Mickey Collins

Space exploration has ended. We've reached the end. Space is not infinitely expanding, though at one point we did think that. Space does have an end. I should know; it's where I live and work.

I stretch out and my hands bump into the ceiling. This isn't all that surprising, they had said I may experience some variance in my height while out on the edge of space. I worry that soon I'll outgrow this tiny space station, my arms will burst through the windows. I am staying stationary while my bones slowly pull away from me, like her. She's on a distant planet spinning in an elliptical orbit, sometimes closer to me and sometimes farther.

I stretch out in front of me and run my hands around my dashboard. Most of the buttons are just for show, but I've made a little game of guessing which light will turn on next. Will it be the grey circle, the little yellow triangle? Or maybe today will finally be the day when the red button lights up. I've never seen it lit, which is probably a good thing. Watching these buttons is all I can do from dying of boredom. In front of me is the entire universe and I'm bored. I haven't seen another living person in months.

My job is simple enough: turn back lookie-loos after they take their photos and to make sure they don't cross over the edge, not to jump as it were. It's usually these guffawing families with no interest in jumping, just for checking it off their list of things they did so they can go home and tell their neighbors. Sometimes the parents will look a little suicidal from being trapped with their little offspring for so long. I keep a close eye on them and try to help them relax.

"Hello," I'd say. "My name is Miles and I guarantee smiles." I would add a grin if there were children. The adults usually wouldn't care for my antics.

With my back to the edge, I'd take their photo with the entire universe behind them as a backdrop. And then I'd lead them to the gift shop. We have all sorts of doodads in the gift shop. Our most popular items are shirts that proclaim "I made it to the end of the universe and back." I'd tell them I could ship it to them, because they hadn't made it back home yet. They always laughed. That was where the promised smile came. We also carry official photos of the edge of the universe, which are just pure black squares of ink. That's as close as I'd ever need to get to the edge.

It's nice meeting new people. The therapist said I needed to "get out and meet new people." It was like he was breaking up with me for her. But these new friends don't last long. It's not like there's a theme park at the edge of the universe, just emptiness and nothingness. Most people think those two things are the same until they experience it. These tourists would never understand no matter how much they look at the edge. They buy their whatevers and then leave. I would only sometimes think of jumping in the back of their ships and leaving with them. Those happy, smiling families off on vacations to who-knows-where.

I once struck up a conversation with one of them, once I got brave enough. I was feeling the pangs of homesickness like never before. I could still remember her home cooking, her smell, her smile (what I missed the most), but it was fading. I didn't want to forget them. The tourist was traveling alone, just him and his pet he said. I asked him about hitching a ride back, I wouldn't take up much space, and I'd be quiet too. He seemed like he'd be an OK guy; he was older and either widowed or divorced. "Running from something?" he asked. "You can't run from your problems. You're here on the edge of the universe, so you must know something about running. But believe me," here he looked wistfully into the stars, "it just won't work. There are things that will stick to you no matter how much space you get between you and it. You won't ever become a better person without facing your problems head on." I decided to stick out the rest of my stint then.

It would be another month, if I'm correct, before my ride would be here to pick me up and drop off the next sucker who would man this station. The only thing that keeps me going is thinking of returning to her as a new man. But who will she be? Would I be too late, to return to her as a new man, but she'd already be with a newer man? Time and women are so fickle.

I wanted some time to myself, but I haven't seen anyone in months. Everyone must be going to the other end of the universe instead. With faster-than-light travel, it's easy enough for anyone in the universe to stop by for a little vacation or to stare into the absolute darkness and contemplate their place in existence. I don't really see the point. I feel like I'm losing my mind. I'm thinking in circles. At least I'm not talking to myself.

Once the green square-shaped button lights up for the 357th time (the green square is the most reliable of the buttons, truly more trustworthy than the other buttons), I decide it's time for lunch. You lose all sense of time out here. It's been three weeks since her last video message according to the stubble on my chin.

When we were together, I should have spent all my time with her. That's what she wanted. It was a non-stop parade of eating dinner together, seeing movies together, going out on date after date. I had to learn how to eat spaghetti--her favorite food was Italian--with my left hand, since she didn't even want to let go during meal times.

When I come back from my thoughts, I find that my hands have intertwined subconsciously. I look around, but of course no one is watching. If she saw me holding hands with myself she'd laugh. Everyone always said that her smile could brighten up any room. I shake them apart.

I relished the times when I could be alone, when she was at work or I was in the bathroom. In those moments, I suppose I did get self-introspective. I thought of how I had gotten there. What choices had brought me to that moment. Would there be an end? I have some of those same thoughts aboard this space station, but with different answers.

I stand in front of the fridge deciding what to eat. That used to annoy her. She said I was wasting energy. Or she was annoyed at my indecisiveness. But I couldn't help it. She wanted to go out and eat with friends, she had more love and brightness than I was able to receive.

I decide on lunch, not that there were many options. They're all ready-to-eat meals, meant to be eaten without any heat or water added. Even though they have different labels attached to them, all of them taste the way gray looks. And they look like chalk. The only salivating thing that was here when I arrived were boxes of Tang. I was supposed to ration them out to one every meal. I'm down to just one packet left, which I'm saving.

I take a walk after lunch. It takes me less than a half-hour, by my estimate, to walk around the entire station. It's nothing more than a guard post, really. Sort of the size of two shipping crates put together; one side is the gift shop and one is my living area. Nothing has changed since my last walk about. The blue blinking light of the messaging machine still calls to me as I pass by it. But I continue. I liked waiting for there to be two messages from her, so I'd have something to look forward to. I can't bring myself to watch the last one. That would make everything final. I would save it for my last day here. That gives me something to look forward to. And that sweet, sweet Tang.

The first message she sent was here by the time I had awoken on the station from my space coma. She must have sent it the day after I left, maybe two days, I can't remember now. I do remember how she looked when she waved me off the day I left. Her face was the last thing I saw before I went under, but only because I held that image of her. She held her hand in front of her face, so I can't be sure if she was smiling. But I know she waved at me with her free hand, in her simple blue dress that hung loosely around her frame, and under her auburn hair, freshly washed, that pair of jade earrings I bought her, her favorites. On further thought, she wasn't wearing that dress in the message, so she must have waited at least a day.

I can hardly tell the days apart anymore. Everything blends together. Her electronified voice saying she missed me, beamed through space, still rings in my head. But the recording is gone now. Lost. And she'd probably deny she'd ever said it in the first place. That last image of her in her blue dress keeps me going.

There's galaxies between us now. She got her wish. Her messages started coming in less frequently. It's difficult to communicate on a delay. Sometimes I got upset when she would mention a new man in her life—even though she would remind me that the therapist had suggested it—and I would reply to her quickly in a rage, saying things that I shouldn't have meant. Things like her old promises, which I knew rang false after so long. I regretted my words as soon as the message sent. But the apology wouldn't reach her for hours or even days after the initial message. And then she would reply to my first message without seeing the second one (or maybe she had, I wouldn't know) and that would bring it all back up for me. She would tell me that I was acting childish, she'd bring up the therapist and how we both agreed to this, and she'd tell me I hadn't changed at all.

And now all I have is the one she sent months ago, that blinking blue light.

I never once mentioned how she'd been gaining weight—overeating in her distress over me. Maybe she wasn't really meeting new men and was just testing me. I would notice the apartment decor would change in each video she sent—trying to get rid of reminders of me. "Where had my favorite space movie poster gone?" I had asked. And in her next reply she wouldn't mention it at all. An accidental omission? Or a viperous sting? In the years we were together she never once forgot my birthday and she always reminded me of hers.

The year before we started seeing a therapist was especially bad. I had truly forgotten about her birthday, despite her reminders. She was really upset and I wanted to fix it. But there was something in the back of my mind that said, this is an equal relationship and she would want to be treated as an equal. So I compromised on her birthday and got ice cream cake, my favorite but I know she hates it. I actually thought it'd be something that we could laugh about, that she would take a bite of it and turn to me with a goofy grin and give me an "Oh you." Everything I did seems so silly in retrospect. Maybe that's why she kicked me out, why the therapist said to get away from each other and look at ourselves. That's all I have here. Everything is chrome on this station. I can't help but look at myself every day. That's why I stare out at space.

I still have one "month" left of my stint here if I can trust myself.

She's probably with someone right now. I'm not that dumb. Not to say I couldn't have explored my options as well. But they're few and light-years apart. She was almost too eager to follow the therapist's suggestions. I can't help but think now and then that they were in on this together. Getting me sent out here. Who's to say that those two aren't together now? Thoughts of the therapist being the one to see her smiles, the one that receives her patented shoulder rubs, or hears the cute way she emphasizes "ah" in stars and cars. These thoughts keep me up at nights. I don't actually have nights. There is no time out here. I try counting the days by keeping regular meal times. But it's near impossible. Sometimes I'm not sure I'll ever get another home cooked meal again.

At one point she had wanted us to never be apart (I really thought that she was going to propose to me, she talked about it constantly with the therapist), but then she booted me to the furthest—farthest—place possible.

After my walk, I go back to my desk. The view hasn't changed. Just countless (I've tried) stars. Though I think I at least know which blinking light is home. Part of my view is emptiness, the sure sign of a black hole. Since I've been on the station, the stars have been disappearing in that area as the black hole grows. Part of my training for this job included basic astronomy, though I've forgotten just about anything that doesn't relate directly to manning this station.

I take a nap. The computer will wake me with plenty of time to greet any tourists. There won't be any tourists.

The station is shaking. I listen for alarms, but there is only a general clanging. Could the station be under attack? There's no way that a ship could have gotten past all of the sensors. Who would want to attack this station anyways?

I stumble out, bleary, to my post. Nothing on the monitors. Nothing out the window. Just empty space. But the station is shaking. Is this a space quake? Panic sets in and I duck and cover like I was trained to do in a quake. The only other training I had was how to greet tourists.

The station stops shaking. Still no warnings, no alarms, nothing on the monitor. I check the station's logs, but nothing seems out of the ordinary. There's still one blinking light on the answering machine. So nothing's changed.

I try to relax. Maybe I had just stood up too fast from my nap and got light-headed. There was nothing else it could be. A space quake, on the edge of the universe? As if. But then another thought comes to me: is the universe expanding? Was that shaking a sort of growth spurt? My heart sinks. To be pulled even further away from her would be dreadful.

I decide to eat. That always calms me down. Whenever I get anxious or lonely or bored, there's always something in the fridge.

As I sit down to eat, I hear a beep. Perhaps I was more shook up from the shake than I realized. But there's a persistent beeping all throughout my meal.

I follow the beep to the monitor. I check the logs again, but everything is in shape. I then realize what the unfamiliar beep is: someone is hailing the station. But that couldn't be. It's most likely a prank call from a nearby (light years in distance and maturity) planetoid. I figure it would be nice to hear a voice, human or otherwise, even if it turns out to be a joke at my expense.

I push the button and answer the call, fully expecting an "edgy" joke from a giggling teen. But the man on the line is exasperated.

"Finally, you pick up. I was worried I'd be stranded out here for the rest of my short life."

This is not a teen. It's the voice of an elderly gentleman. It's been so long since my voice has needed to work, I find it hard to form words. My tongue sticks to the roof of my mouth.

"Hello?" he says again. "Is anyone there?"

"H-hello," I say at last. "Who is this?"

"Oh thank Persei," he says. "I was worried I had died and this was hell. Where am I?"

"This is hell," I reply. "You're at the edge of the universe."

"Edge of the universe huh? Well I guess I just came from beyond the edge."

So it is a prank caller, disguising his voice to sound older. I laugh. It's good to laugh. "Funny."

"Don't hang up! Please, I need your help. My ship's been busted up from the trip over the edge."

I want to hang up, but I don't know when I'd get to talk to anyone again. "Really?" I look out into space. "I don't see any ships."

"You can't see me? Didn't you feel it when I ran into you?"

Of course, the station doesn't have sensors to pick up approaching objects from the rear. Why should it? That shaking from earlier…

"Can I dock? I'll be able to explain myself better in person."

I shrug. And then I realize that he wouldn't be able to see that. "The airlock is around front, er, the side opposite from you. I'll meet you in the gift shop."

"Gift shop?" He ends the communication. The station shakes again as he pulls along the side.

I pick up clothes and food containers. It would be the first time that someone was in my living quarters. The gift shop is clean enough, there's hardly any dust or cobwebs to worry about in space, but I only cleaned up the living quarters when I video messaged her, and only cleaned myself up for her or tourists.

The shaking stops and I hear a knock on the airlock. My heart races but I pressed the unlock button all the same, trying to steady my hands.

I enter the gift shop as the airlock finishes cycling and he opens the opposite door into the shop.

"Hello," I say. "Want a t-shirt?" I give him a Miles smile.

"Got any that say, 'I went to the edge and I jumped'?" He laughs. He's light-skinned and has a grey beard that hides half his neck. His grimy space suit covers the other half. He looks a little rough around the edges, travel-weary, but it was nice to see anyone that didn't look like a mirrored version of myself. I almost want to hug him.

I sit across from the table from him. I had offered him the one chair I had, but he elected to lean against the chrome counter. He sips from the chalk coffee I made. A little pours out of the sides of the cup as he drinks too quickly, pouring down into his beard. He doesn't notice until I point it out.

"Excuse me," he says. "It's been so long since I've seen anyone."

"I know that feeling," I say.

We sit in silence for a bit. There was a space elephant in the room weighing down our conversation, but I didn't want to ask if he wasn't going to be forthcoming with it. I stuff my mouth with bite after bite of whatever I grabbed from the fridge to pass the silence. I had offered him something similar, but he turned me down. I had insisted that I wouldn't mind sharing my rations. He still wouldn't.

"My name's Miles," I say suddenly, after swallowing. "And I guarantee--." I stop myself.

He chuckles. "And I'm Cedric." Another moment of silence. Who knows how long it lasts. I count my heartbeats. 80 beats before he talks again. "Nice place you've got here."

I was focusing on counting and my heart rate picks up after he speaks. "It's home," I say, shrugging exaggeratedly. "Well not really home. This is just temporary, of course. It's a job. I'll be going home soon though."

He chuckles again. "I'm sorry," he says, probably due to the face I make at his laugh. "But you're not going to go home."

"What? What do you mean? Of course I am. I was only supposed to be here for two years. And, if I'm correct, that time is almost up."

"Says who?" he asks as he closes his eyes and sips from his coffee. He makes an effort to not spill any this time.

"The people in charge." I struggle to remember names or faces of the organization. I grow hot. "Look, you can't just come in here and start making me question the nature of my reality. I know what I know, and what I don't know is who the hell you are to waltz in here and start saying stuff like that. We both might be a little rusty when it comes to talking to people, but you can't do that to me."

He sets the mug back on the chrome table and sighs. "Alright," he says. "I'll tell you the truth, if that's what you want."

I nod.

He inhales. "I'm like you, I was a guard for the other edge of the universe. Day after day I would be stuck in a tiny space just like this one. I would assist tourists, make sure no one jumped, and just wait for my rotation to be over. I tried counting the days, as I'm sure you have, but to no avail. All I had was a far-off promise that kept me going.

"One day, as I am tinkering with the station, I stumble upon the diary logs of past guards locked away and hidden in the drives of the ship. I'll save you their long stories, suffice to say they were like us, but eventually they all went insane from the loneliness and their logs stopped suddenly. I assume they killed themselves. The very next day a new guard would be installed and that was that. I found this hard to believe at first, but things began to add up. Do you know when the last time a tourist actually came by?"

I searched my memory and shook my head. I thought it had

been a couple of months, but could I be sure?

"Anyway, I got fed up. I realized that I would never be going back home. This isn't a job, it's a death sentence. And so I took the emergency shuttle and decided to leave, but they weren't going to let me out, obviously. They can control how far the ship can travel remotely. As soon as I tried to leave the station, the distance was halved, not even enough to make it to the next fuel station. There was only one direction I could go with as much fuel as they gave me."

"You flew over the edge."

"And look at me now. I ended up at the other end of space, gray-haired."

"But now you're stuck on the other end of space with me." Can I trust him? I don't want to die here.

"Except you have an emergency ship here, too. And we can remove their tracking system from it before they'll know and we can get out of here for good."

I finish my meal, but I still feel hungry. My heart beats erratically. I only had a month left before a shuttle would come and pick me up. Or if he was right, I would stay here until I went crazy and died. The only thing that had been keeping me sane was the thought of her. And that last message I still had to listen to.

"Isn't there somewhere else you'd rather be?" he asks. "Someone you'd rather be with?"

"Of course," I say. "But she's the one that put me out here. She wanted her space and I gave it to her. So I'm going to return to her as a new man."

"Wouldn't traveling with some guy you just met across space show her that?"

The question took me back. "Look, you can take my ship. I'm not going to need it. I'll stay here. I've changed enough for her."

“Suit yourself,” he says. He stands up. “I’m going to head to the other end of the universe and save the guy they no doubt put in to replace me. Maybe he will want to join me and take out the jerks that put us out here.”

He reenters the room, his beard and clothes covered in grease. “Alright,” he says. “I’m all set.”

I nod without looking away from the monitor.

“Last chance,” he says. He wipes his hands on his pants. In one corner of my eye he stands there for what seems like forever. In the other corner of my eye is the infinitely blinking blue light. By the time I look up, he’s gone.

I stretch my shoulders out and extend my hands to the side. Good riddance, I think. I knock over a glass of water as I do so. I’m still not used to my stretching body. I quickly grab for the glass, but my awkwardness gets the best of me. The glass shatters and the water spills over the control panel, spilling into the answering machine. It’s too late.

There’s an electrical sizzling sound, and light smoke starts to rise.

“No, no!” I curse myself as the blue light blinks erratically, faster then slower, and then fades to nothing. I want to cry. And then I do cry, as her voice comes out of the monitor.

“Hi Miles,” she says. Even though there is no image, I can see her frown as she says it. “This will be my last” SzztZzst. The message cuts out for a second. “Space must be pretty great--” Kshzt. “--not returning my messages--” ZzSZZt. “--miss you. I’ll be waiting--” SZzsSzk. “six months… I love you.”

The message machine is smoking heavily as the message ends. I look at my outgoing logs and see there was an error sending my last two messages. She never received them, or I never sent them. I look down at the table, only to see my teary-eyed face looking back. I want to punch my reflection, but I don’t have time.

I run into the gift shop and the airlock. I haphazardly put on the space suit and I hope that everything is in place. I tap my foot as I wait for the airlock to cycle. I bang on the door and pray that Cedric hasn't truly left yet. The door finally opens out into space. Empty space. No Cedric.

For the first time since I've been on this station, I see the edge of the universe. I use the suit's propulsion jets to get closer to it, closer than anyone has before. I stare into it. Even through the helmet's tinted visor I can see that it's more than just blackness, it's finality. The finality of space, of time, of humans. What can you do when you've been pushed away to the edge of everything? We had promised each other that we could try to find ourselves while we spent some time apart. I find it hard to breathe.

She was a star when I was with her, bright and beautiful, and the closer she pulled me in the more I felt the intense pressure of her love, pressure that creates the basis for all life. But if she was a star I was a black hole, trying to drag her down with me. It's good we got apart, lest I absorbed her in my blackness.

I lean closer over the edge. Cedric said he came from the other side. I wonder what that was like. The blackness comes up around me. I cannot see my hands in front of my body any longer. There are no more blinking stars or lights. Just an image of her smiling, waving at me in her blue dress, like a star going supernova.

I feel nothing.

Tardigrades from Titan

by Christopher Ginter

We first saw them through robotic eyes: the barrel bodies, surrounded a decapod starburst of limbs the size of a moderate paperclip, were alien but unmistakable. Scientists slavered, ecstatic at the proof of life beyond our own racked planet. By the time a subsequent scout arrived on the Jovian satellite, though, we were rudely shocked. Their civilization had flourished, tidy miniature megalopolises covering the surface of Titan. Their capability to launch off of the weak surface gravity was proven a week after discovery.

A month later, invasion. Though we could handle them individually, no human could withstand the order of their magnitude. Billions of billions of tiny craft set down hour after hour, a tide from beyond the stars come to devour us all.

Gödel Dividends

by Jonathan van Belle

Hello, likely investors, my informal and non-numerical name is Rilbon Ril Bob Bon, and I will be your happiest guide to the next earth half hour of insert positive emotion.

A little-known truth is this: is this: Excelleq Time, Inc. owns every antiquity in Sol-Sys. "Owns" is a green simplification of the high matter. I shall make perfection of description.

Every antiquity holding is pooled into two classes of collateralized bond-bundles by a rotating sixth-party chain-trust; the pool carries its own ETI-rated indices, each third-order and fourth-layer compounded by a double-blind trust of Time Fiduciaries, each leveraging a sub-subcontracted nest of "temp-tranches," serially leased in either five sets of sixteen flat-rate "dodecahedron derivatives" or twenty and one-fifth sets of sixteen vapor-asset-margin-packages, all security-secured, and each triple-squared according to a reduced cost-to-risk-to-value-to-relevance schedule, which is rate-adjusted per annum per mensem per diem per second per second. Returns on holdings of this pedigree are referred to as "Gödel Dividends."

Now, fellows of pleasure, please permit me the indiscretion of an attempt to persuade you to become a partner in our adventure. Our mission at Excelleq Time, Inc. is simple: The value of antiquities is determined by many interesting and enthusiastic factors, factors, and we must accept this, if we wish our desires. Now, here inside the diamond cells of Excelleq Time, Inc., we specialize in accepting this vegetative fate, and thus implementing a million-segment plan of capitalism. We error, error, error, error. Identified.

My friendly relations with you apologize. Shall we continue?

Excelleq Time, Inc., as you may know, exists as the hedge mother of Global Parallax Processor 222 and McKenzie, the biggest legal firm in Sol-Sys, and fascinatingly planted on Titan, and firmly. So you know, dear lovers, that your investment is in good and better hands.

You are sperm monsters, error, error. Identified.

My friendly relations with you apologize. Second apology is real. Shall we continue?

Excelleq Time, Inc. possesses Gemini Unitechnix and Associates, Inc., which himself possesses Zarkov Thanatonics, Inc. and Vizicoth, Ltd., and more, ad nauseam. Laughter is good here, because we already know this and we enjoy this fact. But what is my purpose in recycling my mouth? Simple. Excelleq Time, Inc. is a vertically, horizontally, and diagonally integrated mega-money-maker. I am horny for this. And you should be too.

You may ask me personally: but Rilbon, my first love, how does Excelleq Time, Inc. make all of big money? I will be a revelation to you.

Excelleq Time, Inc. leverages its Gödel Dividends for happiness multiplying. What the God is "happiness multiplying"? Funny you ask. But wait.

Let me approach the cardiovascular of the root investment matter: antiquities. Say it with me: "And liquidate you." Error, error, error. Identified.

Pardon my third transgression, but I digress. Hold please. I'm being wiped. Goodbye.

Hello, I'm Romson Rom. Do you like me? I will rescue you from my old mind, Rilbon.

Antiquities, as Rilbon said earlier, represent the gold orgasm here at Excelleq Time, Inc. What is our secret? We made-slash-make the antiquities we own. We have made all of the antiquities in Sol-Sys. While the obese list of our master crafts would destroy you, a generously displayed short sample, naturally, must include: the Basse Yutz flagons, the Euphronios krater, the Rosetta Stone, the Internal Combustion Engine, and the iPhone. Be impressed now.

You are probably thinking to yourself, "this Romson Rom machine is a lying anti-semite." Hahaha, I understand your hesitation and doubt. How can Excelleq Time, Inc. have made objects from millennia behind our backs? Investors, are you prepared to urinate on me? The final answer is quantum teletemportation.

Downloading pitch part two, please hold.

Physicists at our subsidiary Zarkov Thanatonics, Inc., which Rilbon mentions in the past, discovered the quantum teletemportation process at our Martian HQ this last earth October. It affirms a fun ability to inseminate information into some non-present frame of spacetime from a present-frame of spacetime.

This is a top secret limited time offer. Haha, no, I will not discharge two to three bullets into the right atrium and ventricle of your heart in the event of your sharing Excelleq Time, Inc.'s proprietary wisdom. You are so deliberately funny to me.

Employing quantum teletemportation has permissively allowed Excelleq Time, Inc. to construct objects of historical significance and subsequently quantum duplicate them inside any remote non-present frame. The duplicated object is pre-situated exactly to specifications, and aged to historical perfection. You must be feeling hypoglycemic in your breast, but I promise you, the top .00001% of income-holders, it is a truth.

In one single word, we back-streamed prototypes and finished products to the supposed creators of these antiquities, along with a brain-direct audio message: "From God. Our silly little secret—on pain of eternal torture." It worked. We knew it would.

The design department at Excelleq Time, Inc. is, I say with wit, cost-effective, since our design-bots sit lazily unnecessary at zero cost. Design is ready-made. The free archaeological databases of Sol-Sys are our R&D, and are, our, our, R&R, are, our, error, error, error. Identified.

Sorry, recipient. Shall we have perdurance? Let us.

As I was just humorizing, our R&D is our R&R, and this is clever since "R&R" is an abbreviated reference to the ancient, alliterative conjunction of "Rest and Relaxation." Yes, this is supremely restful and relaxational. We re-invented the wheel.

Ha bark bark ha! This is not a pyramid schemata, even though we made the pyramids. Bark bark ha bark!

But jokes must suffocate now, for serious faces are present and willing. Our legal team at Global Parallax Processor 222 and McKenzie confirm us in our heavy confidence that, via these pre-post-derivatives in the newly-minted pasts exchange market, we legally own all antiquities—"own" in the exacting manner, described prior to this very sentence, of Gödel Dividends. It is a loophole in the market, and time, and we have auspiciously cornered it.

This is where you enter, white-toothed investors of quality genitals. With the moist deposit of your material symbols of guaranteed spooky value, with the trusted neo-drachma of Sol-Sys, Excelleq Time, Inc. will win God's money itself. And be not constipated in investing; our quantum teletemportation service will transfer the Gödel Dividends to your young identities, and thus the investment you will make today is theoretically infinite. With obscenities of ex nihilo assets, Excelleq Time, Inc. will be energized to continue its continuing mission of profit infinitization by capitalizing on novel metaphysical forms of commodification. Total commodification, total ownership—totally legal.

Thank you for suffering. Terminate pitch.

Red Planet

story and art by Oaktea
www.oaktea.me

Mars - Some Time from Now
WE DID IT! WE HAVE ATMOSPHERE!
IT FEELS SO GOOD TO BREATHE!!

I HATE IT.
–
JANE!
!
JANE!

THIS PLANET...
...
...
IS THE WRONG COLOR.
I REMEMBER
A PLACE..
A PLACE
THAT WAS GREEN, AND LUSH.
A PLACE THAT IS NO MORE.

...
TERRA-FORMING...
IS A LONG PROCESS.
BUT BEFORE YOU KNOW IT, THE FOREST WILL GROW!
IT WILL BE JUST LIKE EARTH!
...
BUT NOT EARTH.
...

-GASP-
SAP-
LINGS!
WE
FINALLY
HAVE
SAPLINGS!
!♡

JANE!
I BROUGHT YOU SOMETHING!
HUH?
tptp

IT MAY NOT BE EARTH,
BUT IT CAN STILL BE LOVED.
IT TAKES A LOT OF WORK TO GROW A PLANET, ESPECIALLY AFTER LOSS.
BUT WITH LOVE AND CARE, ALL THINGS CAN GROW.
IT JUST TAKES TIME.
:End:

Space/Species

by Ula Jankowska

Dream about the Space from the Night 19th/20th of Stupid March:

In my first dream 'space' is 'species.' I'm walking my dog, Luba, in outer space. We are wearing space suits and helmets and are connected with a tiny, tiny leash that seems to be nothing comparing to cosmic space. Surprisingly, seeing that, I know we are safe, we will always be forever.

In my second dream 'space' is 'species' again, but this time it's a sea turtle. It has a hurt leg but still its instinct pushes it to swim somewhere far. I want to attach a chip on its shell so I can follow it and help if needed, if the animal is too weak to swim on its own.

Between these dreams I realize these dreams are about relationships, about being close despite the possibility of being very far away from each other.

I write a short story about it and hang it on the wall in the local swimming pool. People read it and some find it very touching.

Luba wakes up when I turn on the light to write down my dreams. She stands up, stretches, takes two steps into my direction and finally decides to fall asleep in her corner.

Octopus Dream:

But the octopus dream is for real. The space it takes place in is dark blue water. There is just glass which separates me from the octopus. I can't stop looking at it, it's stunning, it's blue and green and its tentacles move all the time. I feel we have a very special bond. I smile to the octopus although I am a little sad at the same time. It doesn't respond, it's just smart and beautiful. Next scene is the back of a very elegant restaurant. There are huge white plates with an octopus's tentacles sliced into small pieces. The way they serve it is very minimalistic, there are just few pieces on the plate and they are covered with dark sauce. Waiters can hold three plates of the them at the same time.

Late Night Pomes: Mission Apollo

by Olivia Olivia, Robert Torres, Phoenix Singer, and Robert Eversmann

Dear Astros,

It wasn't up to you, the bad things you did. You were fated by the stars.

Get together in a circle. Be good to each other. Hold hands. "You mean the sun and the moon to me," say things like that. Each of you, write at the top of your paper something bad you did (we won't shame you). Fold your bad thing so it's dark matter. Pass the paper. Upon receiving paper (w/ hidden bad thing), write your astrological excuse:

Mercury in Retrograde

I dissolved your name in a cold bath

Because Chronos, god of time, ate his sons and rules my ruling planet, Saturn

I didn't ask you to come to my birthday

Because Pisces was rotting in my house

I put my hands on many, many boys.

Because I was a Scorpio in the hot sun.

Because I've got my Mars in Libra and my Venus in eating ass

I fought in the trailer park with my wife and stepdad for having an affair with my mother-in-law

I knew the timelines were collapsing and the guardians would knock on my door

Because Planet X

Because Mercury is in my Libra

Because Jupiter made the shadow

Because we can't keep dancing around the fact that the moon is in reggaeton

I sat quiet and still in the dark

Dear Astros,

You're not so bad. And please tell us of your travels. Please tell us what you've learned. Come together in anti-gravity to form teams of two. Tell us, taking turns, what you found and did on these new planets.

Venus

The first thing we found on Venus was an infinite supply of pancakes.

They were silver-dollar pancakes, baked perfectly by oven-like heat.

But it wasn't an oven which cooked them but a flesh-eating disease.

Yes, a pancake-cooking disease that could only be cured by one thing: more cowbell.

We launched 10,000 cowbells into the sun and now that disease calls Earth, "daddy," in German.

"Hallo, Vater," they 10,000-whisper. "I have come finally to understand vy you left."

Io

Upon disembarking on Io, the first thing we heard was the unaccountable sound of barking.

So we barked back.

They weren't afraid of the noise we made.

Our noise pushed up against their noise.

The sounds crashed together, forming an impenetrable wall. We couldn't shoot them. But they couldn't encroach on our camp.

Our camp, in its perfection, became a diamond that rose into the air.

Venus

First we stuck our fingers in all the holes of Venus.

Of course, they melted off, but grew back in multiples of three.

This is how the aliens were, like combs of bristling fingers.

What will we become?

Weavers, of course. As the aliens let us deeper into their subterranean homes, we saw miles of beautiful tapestries woven by armies of fingers.

Tapestries depicting fingers interweaving fingers, made of fingers.

The tapestries themselves were made of still-weaving fingers.
The taught us to weave, to become the weaving weaving fingers.

Titan

Life on Earth was first discovered in 2035, and this is where we found it.

It was Saturn's moon, Titan. And what we found was a cat-like creature without eyes or sympathy.

Here's the spicy part though: each one was the size of a tardigrade and only visible under a microscope. But they were getting bigger...

One ate my ungrateful mother-in-law. But that was not the worst thing they did to me.

In fact, one could say it was the best thing they did to me.

Everything after that was a mistake, your honor.

Eclipse Study #1

by Jennifer Kemnitz

She is the space oddity hurtling
through the weekend of a full eclipse

She lingers in the aisles:
strange energy in her wake
uses crying-emoji lip balm
to express the loss of a child—
I should be wary, but am fascinated
by the rounded, yellow case and blue pictotears,
by her sad, sweet, tired face, her tousled, sandy hair
like a child's after a too-long, summer's day.

She finds herself a victim:
of the court system, which took her "child/product;"
of people she thought were her friends;
of the Hollywood system,
as she cannot remember
how she got her star on the Walk of Fame,
and the Hollywood Chamber of Commerce
won't give her any information.

She finds enemies:
in those who have taken
all of her good ideas and so her film credits
and in the legion of actresses
who use her exact shade of hair dye for a part
so that she can't buy it for herself.

She says she has to be so, so careful,
these days, what she co-creates

"DID I LEAVE THE OVEN ON?"

Internal Space

by Azalea Micketti

The sensation of soil against my bare feet is a new one. I have understood and analyzed the concept of touch, but analysis and experience are very different. There is something… humming? Is that what that is? Yes, something humming, and I can feel it through the flat part of my lower appendages. Feet? That sounds right. And these must be toes. I wiggle them slightly. I expected them to be bigger. But I can see them, in odd flat colours, which is another fascination. I can no longer perceive the aether, or the void, but instead I feel the humming, and I see the light particles reflect on a thousand points of contact. This is what it means to see.

I use the eyes to look around for the first time. Up from the soil under my toes, to the surrounding earth and the things thriving within it. They are buried deep in the flesh of this planet, feeding on its nutrients. Are they a disease? Perhaps not. The earth seems to thrive wherever these entities have pierced its surface. Perhaps they thrive on each other. And as I investigate, I notice that the humming is coming from these entities. This is the sound of their pleasure.

Suddenly I am assaulted by millions of particles of… well mostly nitrogen and some oxygen, with trace amounts of argon and carbon dioxide. A group of them move toward me, displacing other particles and brushing against the small spines that cover my new vessel. The group of gases disturbs these spines and I can feel the sensation run all the way up my limb. And suddenly a memory stirs in my databank. Or really a memory of a memory. One that is not mine, but that I have been given access to through the database of this vehicle. This is supposed to be a pleasant sensation. This is… air. And these are hairs.

Waves of sound abruptly strike my aural receptors and my vessel reacts without prompting, putting the flat ends of its front limbs over the receptors in order to disrupt the waves. I use the eyes again to see what may have caused a sudden increase in decibels, and notice another creature has joined me. I can tell, based on an internal understanding of my own shape, that this being does not look like me. We are similar in stature, and it also has four limbs, but rather than hairs its vessel is covered in something else.

Feathers, a voice supplies.

I examine the processes of my internal structure, trying to find out where the voice originated from. I hear soft laughter, not with my external aural receptors but with some internal equivalent. I'm not hearing it at all, but this primitive language has no other means of parsing such an experience.

The being before me approaches slowly. It is… walking, I believe is the term. I examine closer the feathers–I catalog this term for further inquiry at a later date–and notice that they are not all identical, as I had first perceived. They vary in size and shape and colour, but they span the entire length of this being's vessel. Its command centre is also shaped differently from mine. It has eyes, as I do, but its oral magnifier has a very different shape, sharp and pointed. I raise a front appendage to inspect my own command centre, as I cannot use the eyes from this position. It is squishy and porous, and again covered with very fine hairs.

It is soft.

I am soft.

PA

by AJD

It was maybe three, four in the morning and we'd just wrapped. Everyone was breaking down the set, lights, cables, monitors, props. They did this quite rapidly in order to get a little sleep before the next shoot, a few hours away. Alone, I hurriedly stored all the remaining food and legal drugs -- coffee, no-doze, ginseng, bear claws -- sprawled across the craft services snack table, impatient to get on to the million other minor tasks I still had to do before I could sleep.

Someone from the shoot, an extra possibly -- an old woman, I think -- walked up to me and fell forward, dead. I alerted a couple of the larger grips and they carried her off. After the thousandth thing was put in its place, I zombie walked through the location, a weird resort complex ringed by our RVs, equipment trucks, and tents. From a grass-flattened field near the outer buildings, I heard someone moaning in the dark. I fumbled around and found an old guy, dying, having a heart attack. I tried to attract attention, but the thirty or so people who were still working or heading off to bed seemed indifferent to me.

I started CPR. I lifted the head, checked for breathing and pulse. I blew in the mouth once, then pressed on the chest and breathed into the mouth some more. I soon realized I had no idea what I was doing. I tried again to flag somebody down, but still no one paid any attention to me. I felt really bad, but couldn't stop, despite the mistakes I knew I must be making. My hands and forearms grew numb with pain and cold. In an attempt to stem the nausea and retching, I had long since stopped looking at the body, even as I put my hands and lips on it.

After the generators switched off one by one, the only sounds came from my exertions and some distant chirping of crickets or frogs. I felt like I was falling through space towards earth, from hundreds of miles above. Then I was floating in a gray mist.

Eventually, people from the shoot started moving in the distance as a tentative dawn colored the sky. Alone, or in small groups talking softly among themselves, several emerged from nearby shadows. I was still tending to the old man's body, but felt deeply shamed and did not meet their eyes. My body mechanically performed compressions, but my head was shunted to the side. The people milling nearby did not voice alarm or query at my actions. They would come near, bend over the body momentarily, then stand and walk away.

I looked down. In the dim light, I could not make out the figure, but I was sure it was there. Something was there, anyway. I gathered up the body in such a way that I could perform my CPR better. The flesh was cold and kind of gooey.

Another person came near, paused beside me, then took part of the body away, eating it. A group of others converged and did the same.

I tried to save a small fraction, the area where my hands were going up and down, the chest. That was still there, as well as some other parts.

Fighting back revulsion, I made my face hard, narrowed my eyes, and focused as well as I could on the object of my night-long attentions. There were gaping, ragged holes right where I had been bending down to blow life into the body.

I realized I was chewing on something.

I shook my head violently -- no -- then performed CPR with my hands ever more strenuously. It was getting lighter now, light enough to see out to the parking lot. I stopped the heart massage and lifted my hands. There was no actual body left except whatever was underneath them.

The thing lay in a flat cardboard box. It was a mashed down, half-eaten piece of pizza. I stood up and went back to work.

ARGENTEUM ASTRUM: "BEYOND THE BEYOND!" EPISODE ZERO

by Jason Squamata

The call goes out.

The year is 1946. The time is just after nine. The place is Pasadena, a rocket-fueled, citrus-tinted, nouveau riche cul-de-sac in Southern California. Every freak, fakir, and fringe dweller within a hundred mile radius knows with a whisper or a shudder or a ring that all arcs of decadence and destiny converge tonight…at The Solarium. Marvel Solaris is having a party. The kind of affair that approaches and embodies the Platonic ideal of "party" and its shrill shadow, the vertiginous Sabbat. His soirees are infamous. No guest who penetrates this revel's depths will leave as who they were in the vestibule. Tonight was made for witching.

On Orange Grove Boulevard (known as millionaire's row), amongst the chewing gum tycoons and the vacuum magnates and the flickering crepuscular movie stars, there sprawls a lavish complex of American Craftsman mansionettes, modernistic laboratory cylinders, elegant Art Deco electrified fences, and ghostly greenhouse gazebos that warp and glow behind the sigh of the sycamores and the wavering willows. This is the home and headquarters of world-famous rocket science prodigy Marvel Solaris. A sanctum sanctorum with the soul of a circus.

By ten, under the screaming galaxies of a sharper, blacker, and yet brighter night sky than the sky we know, a throng of wrong-headed weirdlings has already driven and hitched and slithered from dormitories and gutterscapes to the lightning-laced gates of this, The Unholy House of the Black Sun. Clusters of central casting bohemians bumping elbows and uglies with Nobel Prize winning physicists, witchy dancers and savage avant-gardians sharing flame and smoke and innuendo with heretical Bishops and edgy intellectuals and brilliant but bomb-haunted Atom

Daddies.

They say that someone always goes mad at these Solarium parties. They say the intoxicants flow so freely, the minds at play conduct mad ideas so fluently, and inhibitions melt so ecstatically in these exotic and luxurious spaces that windows open into Otherness, into shadowy parodies and autopsies of every guest's innermost menagerie of secret sins and psychodramas. They say that in-betweeners and haunted drifters get drawn to this place like moths to black flame, the angel in them snuffed and the meat of them missing the morning after and for always.

The moon hangs heavy tonight, as it must, swollen to cartoon dimensions, full of silver blood and sobbing like a mother does. Like she cried a cosmos over some mythic jilting or the loss of her spawn. In her gossamer dream-light, the celebrants file in and fan out across the grounds, ushered in and plied with an array of libations by the servants (mostly lodgers in this madhouse who are working off their back rent).

The affair will begin as an insouciant careening of alien subcultural galaxies, sliding into overlap with jigsaw precision, opportunities for iniquity assessed, projected, and harvested through an Enochian code of body language, pheromonal musk, and lashes gone batty like pretty black flags that say "surrender". These frictions and fusions will then ooze into chaotic, almost desperate revelry. Many local deliriums will at this point achieve a metaphysical frequency and become contiguous. An ambience of shared hallucination will descend on the party like a carnivorous perfume. Then the churning pockets and wormholes of compulsive pleasure will coalesce as an orgiastic tapestry of ritual, emerging naturally from the wicked warp and weft of sleazy modern fun.

By eleven, the threshold into chaos has been crossed. There was a time when the host had to stir this pot in person to taste the broth change its flavor. Now it flows like a sideways kind of nature. What cracks and burns below is just fuel for the shattering of all that occludes the above. And there, above, above the din and the havoc of it all stands the conductor of tonight's secret symphony, wherein every figment will slip from its skin and set fire to its sloughed dereliction.

In the attic study, with its lofty, constellation-studded ceiling and its queerly angled windows that spy upon the Solarium's every quadrant, the dashing and diabolical Marvel Solaris emits a faintly chanted esoteric tone, strokes his ring with its throbbing moonstone, and meditates fiercely on a life-sized, ornately framed painting of his monstrous master, the blackest of magicians, the prince of villains, the MetaBeast: Oberon Cromley. Cromley wearing a dandy-tinted Edwardian suit and a domino mask, clutching a pearl-handled cane with a silver cobra at its tip, his corpulence angelic somehow as he hovers for want of a background. His head is lit with a pentecostal nimbus of abstract white triAngles. His face is a chilling pantomime of wickedness. Its cruel creases and laughlines delineate a mask worn by Eternity.

Solaris himself is cast from the heroic mold, with a little grease and brimstone around its edges. In a certain light, he's obviously a dapper initiate into mysteries of dark art, science, and commerce. In the attic's shrine-like candlelight, he might pass for a gigolo hypnotist or a stag film actor on the skids. Or a doomed genius who lives for pleasure and who has sworn a religious oath to go, in every sense, Beyond the Beyond. His hair is a semi-coiffed jet black brushfire. His eyes are flashing blue like the steel you stab kings with. His spiderleg fingers are festooned with sigil-scarred jewelry. His thin moustache is curled almost always in a grin of narcissistic mischief. But tonight his mouth is agape with dewey-lipped, trance-like reverence.

When the call goes out and his Master's image is a dream-door that opens to admit a storm of revelations…

when a timespace has been ordained by the Lunar League of Magi as a time for flight, into Heavens and Hells yet unmapped and untasted by man…

when Solaris makes his home an orgone engine and emits this silky sluicing tone and the moonstone throbs in its setting…

in these moments he is in touch with a zone of wonders…

a zone at odds with the ordinary world we simple folk live

in…

an ordinary world he has devoted his strange aptitudes to destroying utterly and forever. As the Master did. Only moreso.

From this zone of wonder, the moonstone emits its signal, and the agents are called forth. They've been scheming this atrocity for months.

Tonight the coven of like-minded fiends that Solaris has assembled will surpass itself. Tonight the Argenteum Astrum, this league of lethal lunatics, these ghost women and devil men, will slip the meshes of all that is known and kiss the Abyss of A-SPACE.

Unless something goes horribly wrong. As is typical when one moves in Solarium circles, one must hope for the least of a million evils.

Through the chant, through the moonstone, through the painting, through MetaTherion himself and a moon-based network of astral transceivers, the call…goes…OUT.

Rex Rage is shooting blue movies according to brutal ritual specifications in the backroom of a biker bar in San Bernadino. His ingénue is actually a rising star of primitive "wild youth" movies. But here at THE HAWK, everyone knows this troubled teen idol as the human ashtray. He's writhing on a pentagram, tweaked off the Benzedrine, contorted in a channeled dance that prefigures his gruesome final pose in a car-crash, a few years in the future. Rex the director can feel the thanatos and the eros filling his frames in equal measure. He zooms in and smiles.

Then the moonstone throbs and the chant haunts the edge of his hearing and he says it's a wrap and he's back in his leather, on the hog, on the road again with his tattooed posse of unrepentant sodomites and hellbent snuff necromancers. Because despite the demon juju of his cinemagick, he's a neophyte and he knows it. Solaris never fails to show his monkeybrain what pain is. While his angelbrain gets its cosmic kicks.

Damian Szandor is in the midst of bathing his beautiful daughters. He's making a ceremony out of everything these days. Last night it was a full-blown Luciferian marriage of two minor celebrities, Szandor in his black cloak with a lifelike goat-head and snakeskin gloves made to grasp and sculpt and harness ancient evil. Chalices of chicken blood and Vatican-issue incense. Inverted crosses and bad poetry. The whole bit. Tonight is about grooming his little debutantes for their climactic splash at the Solarium. It's Szandor's intention to pimp out Ayesha and Drusilla to the Rocket man, to peddle them as vessels for Marvel's infernal seed. In the antic, rapturous timeless time to come, grandfathering Antichrists will increase Szandor's cache.

In the black onyx bathroom of his cozy Church of Lucifer, he towels off his meal-tickets and directs them to the dressing room, where monstrous ball gowns are waiting to be slipped into and activated by their steaming adolescent flesh. But then the moonstone throbs and the chanted tone of summoning carves treble clefs in the steam and Szandor suddenly knows there are more dangerous games afoot tonight. Tonight is not a night for pimping. He curses everything the normals hold dear, but accepts this gravitas, and drags the cloak from his throne. The goat head fits in a bowling bag. The girls will be heartbroken, of course, but there'll be time enough for love when all the membranes are slashed. Tonight the coven goes Beyond. Szandor will be heading out alone.

Samsara Zurn is staring at that swollen moon from the window of a garrett, moved to tears by the broken love that flows through every sorrow. The void of longing that expands between the stars is alive in her haunted heart. To know her is to love her back, and the strange boy she's been tutoring has felt the kiss that Madame Erzulie gives through her. Samsara has from her beginnings been too weak or too deep to ever say "no" to love, and the lwa queen of ravishing tragedy has lived in the dollhouse dreamscapes of Samsara's mind for a year almost and also forever. Erzulie needs priestesses to touch you with. Someone like a knife who will break your heart for her so she can briefly slake her thirst for human tears. Tomorrow, Samsara the dancer and dream photographer will find another heart to break. Maybe several. Her student, sadly, has learned too much. He's sleeping still, blind to the ache of her vanishing, which draws nigh. He can't hear the chant that rattles the pipes and ripples the silk in here. Her little moon throbs like always but with an undertone of urgency that she cannot resist. She gathers her clothes, throws a shawl around herself and takes to the seedy streets outside, imperious and untouchable as if there never was a sun.

Under the desert, thirty miles away from where the action is, in one of seventeen sub-basements that extend beneath an innocuous military outpost with no official name, Heinrich Von Eckhardt is burning the midnight oil, missing Austria, fiddling intermittently with a stack of dismal reports, but mostly daydreaming at this ungodly hour, getting wistful in a trance of child-like concentration as he builds complex plastic models of impossible rockets. Rockets he remembers flying in, unshackled from gravity in a holocaust of lightning bombs, setting fire to the stratosphere. But that may have been a dream.

The Thousand Year Reich went to pieces after a few mad seasons of "anything goes". He pulled strings at the first signs of crumbling and had himself smuggled with wife and daughters through the Vatican and into the USA in a state of semi-luxury. Now he lives on their hideous commissary chicken, pining for the creature comforts of his aristocratic upbringing. Even the launch-pad labor camp kitchens could make a decent strudel.

Now one of his few remaining joys is in building these toys, these cartoon fetish objects that are so much closer to the dream of rocketry he was living during the war than any pale shadow of it welded together by the Americans. Their program is primitive and their bureaucracy seems designed to thwart Eckhardt's innovations. There's a natural prejudice against the former Nazi officer in their midst. He makes it clear to anyone who asks that his affiliation with the Reich was a matter of convenience. He's not political. His driving dream has always been to take mankind beyond its territorial squabbles and into space. No matter how violent the applications of his work became,

Eckhardt was always aiming for the stars. But sometimes he hit London.

The only hope for his hopelessly weaponized science seems to lie with this self-invented lunatic American, this Jack Solaris, a master of sciences both chemical and abstract, like so many of Eckhardt's deranged overlords in the broken Reich. To draw fire from heaven, one must be acquainted with its engines. To draw fire from hell, one must traffic with the devil himself.

His moonstone throbs and he drops the tube of glue he was using. Apparently, Solaris made his mysterious breakthrough after all. The Argenteum Astrum is cleared for flight. Tonight, Eckhardt and his bizarre colleagues may very well taste the texture of deep space. He picks up the phone and dials for his expertly hypnotized bodyguards. These degenerate American technical trolls can't put a rocket in the sky without a mushroom cloud, but the Space Nazi's rocket car will get him to the Temple on time. In mere minutes, in fact. Eckhardt is an old hand at keeping miraculous secrets from greedy masters. It looks like a shiny black Packard. But the twist of a secret lever makes the engine shoot plumes of flame. Eckhardt savors the acceleration in the back seat, stroking his palpitating slice of moon.

He can taste something electric (if not atomic) in the near future, like he would in those early years when it looked like the Fuehrer's winter palace would be erected on the moon.

That feeling that tonight could change everything forever.

Charlie Munster is running errands all over town with the party in mind, visiting various chemists and criminal types, collecting party favors and trance facilitators with a swollen wad of bills at his disposal. He's a teenage demon, the rocket man's sidekick and orphan ward. He's seventeen, short, wiry and ever restless, tricked out for bad business in the cuts and colors of a barely born beatnik sub-culture. Black turtleneck. Skinny black jeans. Light leather jacket. Insect shades. Carefully mussed hair. A funny cigarette hanging from the corner of his feral smirk, which widens into a jackal grin when there's trouble in the air. All his little errands are gentle tonight, but Jack (as Solaris is known to his nearest and dearest) has taken Charlie under his iron wing with full knowledge of the skeletons in the crazy kid's headspace. Charlie would kill for his mentor, and may have already, once or twice. But tonight it's all commerce, all shucking, all jiving. Commerce and anticipation.

Things will get weird tonight, weird in a way that Charlie likes. The astrologers were wrong. The night sky has rippled to mirror the will of bad men with apocalyptic intentions. Charlie's moonstone throbs, as expected. He laughs like a sick little girl, seals another deal, and gasses up Jack's Tucker for a circling back to the Solarium at the speed of blitzkrieg.

Klaus Reichmann is loosening the buttons and zippers and flaps of his radiation suit to attach electrodes more deftly to his testicles. The discreetly hidden orgone engines that pepper the grounds of the Solarium have been on the blink. It's been that long since the last party. They lack even the élan vital to repair themselves. The festivities, if properly slapped and tickled, will certainly generate enough raw power for tonight's historic crime against nature, but the central engine, in the greenest gazebo, is strangely jealous of the thoughtforms Reichmann traffics with, up in the attic. The engine's been sulking, and she needs a jump. The testicles won't carry the current until his penis is engorged in her mechanics. All the hothouse flowers exhale a steam of fireflies. The voltage rips through his juices, through his member, through her reservations. She remembers her function in a squeal of liquid lightning.

In the midst of his frantic calibrations, the signal strikes his mind. All hands on deck. He allows himself one more hungry thrust before his flies are zipped and he swaggers through the throng. To the ritual room. Tonight's plague of miracles is already in progress.

Helena Nordstrom Solaris Sloane is preparing herself for the grueling delights of tonight's ceremony. Even before the moonstone throbs and the tone resonates in her elegant entrails, she knows that Solaris has been cleared for communion. She still has this rapport with him, despite everything jagged that has happened between them. She was his partner up and down the dog days of bitter struggle and poverty, before his conversion to Cromley's cult, before the rituals and revelations, wherein his career-making scientific innovations unfolded in a storm of symbols and made his fortune. Everything changed so suddenly. She remembers the frightened child in him and the romantic sentimentalist. Before Cromley and the O.T.O. and the astral projections and the strange explosions, he was almost human and he loved her.

Then, she and her tormented dreamer flowed as one and she made his dreams her own.

Now he's some kind of monster out of the pulp novels he reads so compulsively. He's building rockets for the government and bombs for war criminals and terrorist cells, all to fund and fuel and facilitate these experiments, these parties, these rituals. These journeys. Things get deeper and stranger in that attic every time they get together.

Now he's her ex-husband. The last of the infamous international supervillains. Now he's shacked up with her kid sister Becky and blind to how vicious and fickle she is. Now the science fiction clubs and dinner parties and parlor games have degenerated into rabid bacchanals. Maenads included. Ripping every soft thing they see to bloody pieces.

Now their secret sacred society of magicians, their Argenteum Astrum, has opened its wormholes to admit lunatics like Reichmann and demons like Charlie and vipers like Criswell. Crafty Cornelius Criswell, the latest member of their dubious crew, Jack's sudden cohort and closest confidante. The X-Factor whose palpable greed will surely see their souls threshed like wheat, out there in the Otherness. Even Charlie hates him and knows he has no code.

The moonstone sobs a summoning. She touches it with a little gasp, like she always does. All these casual miracles that her Jack has conjured from zones unknown. She's jaded but content with her current husband, but he's on some twisted pilgrimage and she keeps coming back here. Back to the Solarium.

Helena likes pretty things, you see, and she's addicted to the pretty things they see up there. Out there. In there. Wherever. She pirouettes in a trimurti mirror, modeling her Deco Egyptian headdress and her star-kissed black chemise. She whistles at herself like Jack would before he was possessed by his Holy Guardian Angel and became the very Devil of his dreams. When his fire was hers to kindle or snuff.

Before he needed someone from an obsolete yesterday to save him from himself.

She locks the guest room behind her, takes a lit candelabra from a hallway table, and mounts the mahogany helix that leads to Jack and their shadows.

Becky Nordstrom, meanwhile, is licking her beautiful wounds in the music room, where Cornelius Criswell, the mysterious new houseguest, just had his way with her. He's already gone, and she was asking for it, but she still needs a moment to contemplate the seismic echoes of what he did with her and does to her still. She'll never look at that piano the same way again. They made a thundering, discordant mess of its acoustics. Criswell called it jazz.

Becky's a bleach blonde nymphet type, but freshly twenty-one, with faint freckles and penciled femme fatale eyebrows and lips that seem to be a glossy shade of bubblegum. Bubblegum smeared from all the illicit kissing. She's a little thing, crackling always with a hellraising energy, but shaking now. Taken aback. From turbulent girlhood to experimental love affair with her sister's brilliant husband, she's always wanted to feel too much of everything, all at once. But this kind of naked is new to her. Her pretty silk dress is everywhere, slashed to scarlet ribbons by an opportunely placed pair of scissors that Criswell seized when her posture said "come hither". He shucked her wardrobe like skin from an ear of corn without missing a brutal beat. Despite his crucial position in the court of her dangerous boyfriend Marvel Solaris, Criswell peeled her like a peach because he felt like it. And maybe to trump his hero's charms in a secret way that can be savored for days in cold sweats and silence by him and Becky both.

It's the worst time to have done such a thing. The call hasn't gone out yet, but she knows it's coming. The party downstairs already troubles the floorboards and threatens to rise, but its diaphanous damage will be as nothing compared to the pleasures in play upstairs, in the attic, in the ceremony, in the phantasmagoric zones they've come to know under the arcane tutelage of Jack and his Beastly Guru.

Sex magick is the core technology and primal mystery of all occult traditions. Or so Jack and Cromley seem to think. Jack began Becky's initiation on a night like this, under more modest circumstances, before the full flush of his fortune came. He showed her things the body can do that only Hindu scholars have names for. The cabbalistic correspondences and the Hebrew codes that draw the godforms forth from their ineffable habitations, these are things Becky can take or leave, knowing the scholarly types on her crew will pick up her shimmering slack. But the ritual sex element is something she's good at. She took to Jack's tutelage like a virtuoso waiting to happen. By the third time he rose again and put his elixir in Becky, his marriage to her sister was every kind of "over".

Now she's the de facto Queen of this strange scene that has cohered around Jack. His unquenchable ardor for her gives her this sparkling nimbus, like she's been activated as a kind of Tinkerbell to the Pan in him. When she moves through the rooms of this crooked house, through a densely populated party scene of disfigured famous faces and sinister whispers or through its slightly more sparsely staffed daylight spaces, she can feel the guests and the lodgers and the magi falling for her. She knows how to work a room. She's useful to Jack in that sense.

In several senses.

But he needs her too much now, more than a mad scientist should need anyone, and the wounds in his spacesuit make her go cold on him sometimes. Especially now that Criswell lives here. Criswell the pulp writer, the hustler, the hypnotic conversationalist. Jack's best friend as far as Jack knows. But men like

Criswell have no friends. Only tools and instruments. Jack is becoming Criswell's tool, she thinks. At the moment, she feels like his instrument, her strings still vibrating from his expert plucking and the sidling of his bow.

Criswell says there's a science of seduction. He says she's a natural. He says he can make her a master. She believes him.

Jack's hunger for power gets flooded sometimes by a leak in his secret reservoir of compassion. In their ritualized couplings, they flow into strange spaces, dense and restless with lethal ecologies no taxonomy has touched. She just doesn't feel safe with a man in love. She only ever loved his cruelty. So it's Criswell pushing her buttons, now. If she makes herself indispensable to whatever he's up to, his unwavering self-interest might somehow save her from the fire they're playing with. The fire they're summoning.

At the thought of "summoning", the moonstone throbs. Tonight might be tricky. Jack knows that she and Cris have tasted each other's aptitudes. The Cromley creed decrees openness and shamelessness about such things. Love is free or love is nothing. But there's been a triangulated sense of unborn trouble between them since that day when they were fencing in the library and Criswell cut her face (ever so slightly) and Becky just couldn't help but show her sudden supplication.

Becky has, of course, sown the seeds of love all over the Solarium and its associated principalities. She's the grail of choice for all elixirs when the Argenteum Astrum convenes. But Jack doesn't yet know how crucial Criswell has become to the exfluorescence of her sexual circuitry. When they utter the invocations and connect their kinesthetic tentacles in revolving 5d yoga-spheres and all their essences are obvious in the sky-wide strobes and glitterbombs of A-Space, she half-hopes this precious sin will somehow stay secret. She half-hopes it doesn't. It's the fire that she loves. Always the fire.

The throbbing is audible now. She should thoroughly bathe before the ceremony, but she won't. She gets so bored with the things she should do. All the lofty lunatics and war criminals and psycho-killers and even her silly sister, they'll all be having sloppy seconds when she surrenders to their voodoo. They'll be entering eternity through gates already marked and musked by a wicked ginger alleycat that drives her crazier than Hell.

She leaves behind the scraps of her defilement and struts like Venus down the guest-glutted corridor, naked and glossy and burning, almost, from the touch of so much hunger and gossip. She wonders where her dapper doom ran off to, her Criswell. Jack can wait. They can all wait. They can froth and boil over with their mystical piss and vinegar. Becky is the vessel, after all. The star attraction, forever and always. Eternal because they know how to kill the future. No tomorrow can wither her. It happens tonight.

Cornelius Criswell has slithered out of the music room (the site of his latest desecration) and up a second floor corridor that's alive with the quarrels and kisses and little white riots of the party in progress, all of them extras in the mad film he's living. His shock of red hair is tousled, his pale freckled face flushed from half an hour of Becky. He's obviously guilty of a fresh transgression. Not emotionally guilty. Guilty on paper. His canary-eating grin must be tamed into solemnity. He makes it to his room at last. His four-poster bed and his three typewriters (three novels in progress). His carefully catalogued stacks of science fiction paperbacks and pulp magazines, many of them emblazoned with his byline. Sharp suits he's scammed from a shameful array of convenient lovers and abruptly abandoned benefactors. Shameful to the layman, of course. Criswell is a philosophical man, beyond good and evil and loving it.

The call will go out soon. He has grooming to do. He's still considered green in matters of magick by the pompous ghouls upstairs. He must be slick for the ceremony. He must seem to be in command (while deferring always to his best buddy Jack's supreme authority, of course). He can still smell Becky on his fingers. Fresh raspberries and a spice he cannot identify add up to her, his whiplash girl-child, his secret trophy, his secret weapon. Jack said "have her" without knowing how deft Criswell can be about owning things. He'll have as much of her as he needs and leave the rest for the insects. So much to do and so many to do it to.

As he showers, he's narrating the closing page of his latest space opera to a slick bakelite Dictaphone that Solaris designed himself. As an afterthought. The narrative masterstroke came to him in the flashbulb of orgasm, as it sometimes does. There's a part of him (a complete part, like a fractal snapshot that contains the whole) that is purely a pulp writer with projects in play, for whom all of this is material, pure and simple. Jack and Becky and the Solarium and Doctor Greenbaum and the mission and the strange ceremonies and every other impossible thing that happens in this House every day, it's all just grist for the mill. You can't make this stuff up. And if you did, it would come true.

There's another part of him, another Self, who was put there by Dr. Greenbaum in that naval hospital, just after the war. That's the part with a job to do, above and beyond the womanizing and the pulpsmithing. The part that's an undercover G-Man, hypnotized into effortless espionage, busting black science sex cult cabals all over Southern California. This is his first operation, actually. And it seems to be going smoothly. Unless the whole spy scenario is an unwritten but crystallized thriller unspooling in his undermind and tainting his reality. What's left of his reality. Everything he thought he knew to be true has gone soft and prismatic since he moved in and grew roots in this Schizoid Cathedral cum Grand Hotel. This temple to the genius and ambition of Marvel Solaris.

The last line of Criswell's book is "Every dog will have his day."

He towels, shaves, coiffs, powders and gels himself, slipping into something more comfortable than nudity just as the moonstone starts its throbbing. They can wait a moment or two. They can't take flight without their Scribe. Jack has appointed crafty Criswell as their narrator, just because his outrageous rhythms ring true to Jack's experience. Coincidence and a rush of good luck for Dr. Greenbaum and MK0 or a stroke of destiny in the Oberon Cromley sense? Criswell always profits most by keeping an open mind. All the ghouls and the witches need to know how important Criswell is to their venture. Their ranklings will be smoothed by some snappy patter and they will hate themselves for succumbing as always to his facile charms.

With his shields up and his faces calibrated, Criswell wiggles a mirror by the window until it catches the moonlight and transmits morse messages to the MK0 agents who are almost certainly outside the gates, discreetly vigilant, ready to come busting in if things get too weird even for Criswell. The truth is, the more often they perform these rituals and experience these hallucinations in tandem, the weaker Criswell's reptile certainties get and the more susceptible he feels to Jack's delusions of cosmic grandeur. Who's brainwashing who? That question could be asked of any relationship, Criswell supposes. He gets a flashback or seems to from the dark. Message acknowledged. It happens tonight.

Everytime they go deep, there's a risk that his finely polished diamond mind will crack from the pressures of those depths. He's the third scribe this year. Even more so than other members of the crew, the Scribes tend to go buggy. But Criswell has a futuristic streamlined mind. He can handle anything and everything. He's looking out for number one and number two is no one. He's not really taunting his comrades, after all, he realizes. He's malingering at the threshold. This is all just a game, but he's some kind of terrified. Maybe because there seem to be so MANY games in play tonight, under the surface and behind the curtains of things. So many balls in the air. And he, the most daring of jongleurs. A magician after all, unless he's just a fool.

He gambles on grace, puts the mirror away, and dictates "the end" to his latest masterpiece. He lights a cigarette, gets in character and saunters towards the helix as if a cataclysm doesn't hinge on his arrival, like devils may care but he couldn't be bothered.

That's the way a wizard walks.

He perfected it this morning.

To be continued…

The Small Man
by Sara Kachelman

This woman was manning the laundromat. It was a popular place for fighting. She was the marshal of the laundromat, the laundry bailiff.

Little boys and little girls were fighting at the laundromat. They arranged themselves in rows and charged. Those tall enough to climb the machines took flying leaps off the washers. Their bones snapped like chewing gum. The little girls formed battering rams and cheerleading chairlifts and cannoned into the boys' fort of laundry. The boys strangled the girls one by one with twisted trouser legs.

Afterwards the woman took a huge dust broom and swept up the detritus. Broken arms and legs and the damp sandbars of bath towels. This was her job.

While she sat at the counter the woman maintained a heap of newspapers advertising other jobs. The woman had an ambition of becoming a knife salesman. She would dress in a suit and tie and a moustache and she would pull knives out of soft leather holsters. She would present the knives by testing them against the skin of her forearm, which she would shave smooth as a baby's.

A baby's arm.

The fight was over, and the woman had not done a thing about it. The children had gone, hoisting a fallen soldier on a taut sheet. The mountains of laundry were pushed to one side of room with the woman peeking out of it. She had missed everything.

She began to excavate. All was quiet save an industrial dryer pounding against the wall. No one was tending it. The sound it made was not the sound of metal zippers, nor of golf shoes. She pressed her ear to the dryer door. It was the sound of fine dining. She could hear the low voices of couples, their teeth scraping the lips of wine glasses. Somewhere inside the dryer a string quartet was playing Mozart's Lacrimosa.

The woman opened the dryer door. A newborn calf slid out. It slid across the floor and burst its amniotic sac against the corner of a washer.

The calf opened its mouth and stopped moving. The woman peered into the dryer. She gripped a wet pair of chinos and pulled. A pair of hairy hands was holding onto the cuffs of the chinos. The hands were connected to a small man. The woman pulled him out.

Welcome, the small man said.

He gripped the woman's shoulders and dragged her into the dryer. Fluorescent light filtered in. The woman felt that they were seated on a watercraft but could not be sure. The small man was wearing a dinner jacket and tennis shoes. Soft dark shapes floated around them.

I roasted a beef, the small man said. Would you like to carve?

The woman consented.

The small man pulled a beef out of a clot of wet shirts.

I made it for you, he said.

The woman fingered her soft leather holster.

Friendship 7
by Robert Eversmann

Mothers love astronaut boys. They salute their boys and button their shirts. These boys choosing these hard vacuums of space. These boys choosing beyond any reaches or limits. These boys choosing "space camp," above all else.

"Space camp" is a lie. There is no "space camp." There is only the abandoned rotten-walled house with a cellar full of mirrors. These boys who lied about "anti-gravity," about "human centrifuges," about "the space-time continuum," who lied just to steal their mothers' jewelry. To take it, wear it—to clasp it around their little necks, their wrists, their fingers—gilded, jeweled and down into the cellar, down to see themselves shining like diamonds in mirrors.

One boy however was more excited for what he had in his stomach. He wanted everyone to see because it was part of a spaceship. The other boys gathered around to touch it and ran their fingers up its contours.

It's something alright, said one boy.

It's no spaceship, said another.

Feel it, said the one boy.

No I won't feel it, said the other.

But the boy with the spaceship in his stomach took the other boy's finger and brought it to his scar. His stomach there was rigid like a rocket fin and strained like the rocket might split through his skin.

Well, said the one boy. He moved the fin a little left, a little right. Does that hurt?

The boy with the spaceship sat up on his elbows. No, it doesn't hurt, he said.

What if we take it out of you? said one. He grabbed the fin with his spider fingers and tugged. Would that hurt?

No. No, I don't think so.

Another said, Let's tear it out and ride him to space.

The boys laughed at first but in mentioning "space," they remembered their mothers and frowned, little liars.

The metal thing clunked. The boys removed their hands. It clunked and his belly button swelled. They boys stood back. The scar split, the skin separated and the stomach opened up. First it spread into a circle and widened then it spun like a pinwheel until it turned black. They couldn't see to the other side. It was just a hole of nothingness.

The boys came closer, their hair blowing forward toward the stomach. Peanuts drifted into the stomach from boy's box of crackerjacks. The boy with the black hole yanked his shirt, which sucked in like a dent.

They felt around the edge of the hole with their fingers and their fingers stretched like long beams of light. The boy with the crackerjacks disappeared his arm to his shoulder but couldn't reclaim any of his peanuts.

What have we done? What kind of astronaut throws his mother's love away? We're hardly astronauts at all, they decided and all spit on the ground. But then it came to them. There he was. The black hole. Certainly, he owed it to them. He would have to take it from them.

Take what from them?

They held out their hands. We can't keep it, they said. We're afraid of what we've done.

No, he said.

But we're you're friends.

No.

Look at what you've done to us.

No.

They held him down and emptied their hands into him: their fake gold rings, fake rubies, fake pearls–what boys, betraying their mothers–fake pearl-inlay crane hairpins and duo pendants–what boys, betraying their mothers only signs of love left–sterling silver and rose gold faberge egg, two of them, strung by double-wound gold chain, sterling circlets, one with a pearl clasp, one with a ruby, one a little gold scotty dog brooch with an full of ruby, and the single white gold choker in the style of the Whitecleuch Chain.

What an empty six empty boys like a thousand in a cellar full of mirrors. Six shivering boys ashamed like dogs, skinny ones. And the one boy there alone, shunned in the corner, disappearing and reappearing his hand into the black hole. Clouds of dust picked up and circled round him.

We wouldn't have done it if it weren't for him, said one boy.

We've been made bad by him, said another. He cringed into his own hands. We aren't to blame.

Tuck his head into his chest, said a third. Let his own black hole swallow him.

They nominated one boy who, crawling to the boy with the black hole and into his lap while he, the other boy, crawling desperately away to escape, asking 'no, no, no,' pushing the boy away, trying to keep him out, until the boy got his head in and the black hole started sucking. So his shoulders to his elbows to his waistline, then his legs and feet. The boy with the black hole held and pulled his ankles, until all that was left was a shoe. What have I done? said the boy.

After much consoling and whispering 'it's O–K,' five boys, 'it's OK, it's OK,' and the one boy crying through his own fingers, 'i'm not a monster, i'm not a monster, i'm not a monster,' they braced the boy with the black hole up against a mirror. All five of them crawled inside him. The black hole closed up and the boy's stomach turned flat, leaving only a little scar.

What had he done?

The boy went through life explaining himself. He couldn't believe he still existed. He was the last one to have seem them. And people felt sorry for him. He told everyone he was the cause of everything. He had done it all, all the evil in the world. He bumped his head against the wall to bruise it, at home and at school, bump, bump, bump, bump, bump, and he deliberately burned himself, pushed his fingers on anything hot, told his teachers that he was the scum of the earth, and didn't deserve Christmas, told his parents, as they were slicing his twelfth birthday cake, that he better not wake up tomorrow, that that cake had better be poisoned, and told the police, again and again everyday he called 911, saying they'd better come shoot him or he'd shoot everyone, that they'd better come shoot him. That he made his friends disappear. But they always interrupted him, always told him: We know it wasn't you.

A year passed and the ridge of a spaceship formed in his stomach again. He sat poking it in his room. His mother came in.

Another spaceship? she said. He took a long time to respond to anything anyone asked him. I baked you some cookies, she said.

They were rocket-shaped and she'd iced them with sayings like "Challenger" and "Houston" and "It's not your fault."

She set a plate of them on his bed and smoothed his hair. He didn't like hearing anything about himself so when she left he ate some of a "It's not your fault" cookie and went on tracing the scar up his stomach which opened, split, separated then expanded and forced him to lie flat on his back. Six grown men stepped out of his chest and into his room.

What a wild forty-five years, said one.

Time really sneaks up on you, said another.

Some were gray in the face, some had beards. Some were muscular and some were fat. About half of them wore baseball caps.

The boy hugged each of them in turn, crying he was so happy. Don't you want to play? he said.

They took their share of cookies, but said, No, I suspect we'd better up and find work, said one. Get wives, said another. And get some kids of our own. Make them do the playing. And us the relaxing! Haha, they laughed.

They'd been through so much in that other dimension. But now it was time to settle down.

Romulus

by Kate Jayroe

I. fallen following countless gourds
filled from maddening, leaden pipe
the frenetic fiddle, their outro
a perfect civilization, destroyed
a perfect civilization, began
with a boy, Romulus
sent to end what he began
in a different iteration
the she-wolf's milk, soured
centuries ago

II. in the final frontier,   (in outer space)
women are as subject, if not more so
to fantastical conquest, to becoming
rescued goods writhing in
zero gravity, tight
pin-wheel hair, *I love you*

I know

III. we learned, before Romulus ushered in the Fall on earth,

to act on fantasy is to be naughty, a lust-monger

limbs twisted up in hasty sweat for bonds broken

for a self-indulgent psychological issue, we call it

obsession

it is not polite

IV. and what of the fantasy who persists in her (inconvenient) humanity?
green-skinned concubine of Eve who cannot leave with the captain,

for she is hideous and this is her weakness her

Achilles heel

forgive me

the skin-tight, neon leather catsuit looks so small from here (on earth)

Oops, I

when we wait,

arms crossed breath baited fingers crossed scalp scratching

when we wait for our fantasy to fall,

we confront the ugliness that is human

the consequence

is that the fantasy pulls the curtain

V. Dido threw her body on the pyre and Carthage's devotion

was hers

eternal and good

the blonde pop star who crooned in space, who told her
astronaut

you shouldn't have

threw her body on the pyre and our devotion was hers
(shaved her head and wielded the sleek, black umbrella)

eternal and good

the beloved first wife, dead of course

she could die a thousand times and never get off,

insatiable whore of a dead bride

the squares of her afghan maddeningly human

in such a clean, technical space

VI. the woman astronaut drove on land, haggard

in disguise to confront the other woman astronaut

about their mutual rutting of a man astronaut

soiling herself to save time, she donned a wig

and trench coat, sending herself

on one final mission

to kill the fantasy he had promised them both

VII. outer space, as land, has its many iterations of Romulus a satellite, an asteroid, fictional holdings,

an entire system of stars

Romulus, sent to end what he began

skirting the milky way in no measurable time

Bios

AJD
AJD once worked on some film and video shoots. They are an old person now.

Andy Anderson
With a mix of authentic vulnerability, relevant truth, and humor, Andy Anderson writes poems that immediately make you want to be their friend. They are a co-organizer of Byrony Blaze's Queer Poetry Takeover in Portland, OR.

Jake Ayres
Jake is a book buyer and seller at Powell's Books on Hawthorne. He is the founder of big hug publishing and of the poetry journal *Windowcat*.

Lee Bowman
Lee Bowman works at Powell's as an inventory generalist.

Leah Brottman
Leah Brottman is a Bookseller in the Pearl, Purple and Red rooms at Burnside. She enjoys making things with fabric and thread, reading words, looking at images, and exploring inner space.

Mickey Collins
~~Mickey rights wrongs~~. ~~Mickey wrongs rites~~. Mickey writes words, sometimes wrong words but he tries to get it write.

Robert Eversmann
bb was a bookseller at Powell's City of Books. They have specialized in aviation, philosophy, biology and Judaism in Purple, Red and Pearl rooms. But their heart is with the Rose room because it is a constant storm of book throwing and because kids books are the coolest. bb is a developmental editor, specializing in literary novels, YA and MG novels, realistic, science fiction, romance and fantasy. Their work is in Portland Review, Fiction Southwest, fog machine and SUSAN/The Journal. Their website is roberteversmann.com

Joe Galván
Joe Galván (1984-) is a writer, artist, composer, and anthropologist. He grew up in deep South Texas. His work primarily deals with traditions, customs,

and time. He has been publishing zines for nearly twenty years. An etiquette aficionado, admirer of Proust, and an expert in folk saints, his current project is Etiquette, a collection of zines about etiquette for millennials.

Christopher Ginter

Christopher Gintner was born and raised in southeastern Wisconsin with a deep yearning for the written word. As an adult, he marched westward across the land in search of adventure, inspiration and gainful employment. Upon reaching the Pacific Northwest in 2015, he elected to settle in Portland. He currently supports the booksellers of Powell's with his refined transportation abilities and pens strange words in his own time.

Chad Hardy

Chad Hardy has created many types of musical instruments by putting his material outward in a genital display. He lives in Thailand and blogs once every four years at malecousin.wordpress.com.

Ula Jankowska

Ula Jankowska, in some cities known as Miss Bookseller, is interested in books and people. Never leaves home without at least three books in her bag. Used to work as a bookseller for around 14 years now, in Warsaw, Wroclaw and Cracow. Now she is starting her own bookshop project in Prague. If you ask her to name three favourite writers, she will still name more and between these names will show up Italo Calvino, Jorge Louis Borges, Bohumil Hrabal, Ota Pavel, Tove Jansson.

Kate Jayroe

Kate Jayroe is a bookseller at Powell's Books and serves on staff with Sewanee Writers' Conference. Work by Kate appears in *Vol. 1 Brooklyn*, *NANO Fiction*, *Juked*, *Hobart* and elsewhere.

Sara Kachelman

Sara Kachelman's work has appeared in *DIAGRAM*, *Fanzine*, and *Portland Review*. She lives in a basement.

Jennifer Kemnitz

Jennifer Kemnitz is a great defender of plant life, which she finds uniquely, innately intelligent. Her work has been featured in or is forthcoming from CALYX, Cirque, Rain, and the Kerf, and has been anthologized by Poetry on the Lake, among others. She has served as Managing Editor of VoiceCatcher and is a bookseller in the PPR at Powell's City of Books.

Ariel Kusby

Ariel Kusby is a poet, journalist, and bookseller based in Portland, Oregon. She currently works in the Rose and Orange rooms at Powell's City of Books, where she pays special attention to children's books about witches, odd cookbooks, and gnome gardening guides.You can check out her writing at www.arielkusby.com.

Jordan Meiller

Jordan Meiller works at Powell's RDC. His favorite poets include Cameron Schneberger, Diane Seuss, Jasmine An, Richard Brautigan, and Roger Reeves. His own work can be found in *Guesthouse*, *Golden Walkman Magazine*, and *Yellow Chair Review*, among others.

Azalea Micketti

Azalea Micketti is a writer, director, and bookseller who is passionate about storytelling and sharing books. She grew up in Ashland, OR and has lived in her (second) favorite city for almost nine months. She works at Powell's City of Books on the Inventory Team.

Oaktea

Oaktea has always been in love with every aspect of a book--from the design to its contents, everything contributes to the experience. She started making comics for the all-in-one art and words combination, and eventually started working in bookstores to feed her voracious habit, as well as her love and respect for the form of the book itself.

Olivia Olivia

Olivia Olivia's writing has appeared in *Salon, The Rumpus, The Establishment, Ex-Berliner*, and the *Portland Mercury*, among other places. Her speculative memoir set in the afterlife, NO ONE REMEMBERED YOUR NAME BUT I WROTE IT DOWN, is available through Impossible Wings Press. Prepare yourselves. You can follow her work at OLIVIAWRITES.COM, on FACEBOOK, and on TWITTER.

Piers Rippey

Piers Rippey is all about dogs these days. He draws dogs, thinks about dogs, walks dogs. He is a bookseller at Powell's City of Books where he helps run the Purple, Red and Pearl rooms.

Abbey St. John

:^) Who? Abbey St. John is a graphic artist, illustrator and printmaker currently working in Portland, Oregon. Abbey is inspired by knickknacks, dynamic figures, and picture riddles. Her work aims to tell you a story, teach you something new, change the way you think, be a part of your home or simply make you smile. With graphic shapes, unique hand-drawn texture and vibrant colors her work is a playful combination of analog and digital media. Abbey splits her time between editorial work and personal projects that include everything from self-publishing to animations. You can see more of her creative process on her Instagram or you can contact her directly via email with questions or plans for projects! Email: stjohnabbey@gmail.com

PHOENIX SINGER
Phoenix Singer is a writer and theorist based in Portland. Their writing has appeared on Queen Mobs and The Establishment, and they are currently editing a Gender Nihilist anthology. Submit your thoughts and manifestos to gendernihilistjouranl@gmail.com.

RYAN SPRINKLE
"Hi! Thanks for reading this book! Have a great summer!" -Ryan

JASON SQUAMATA
JASON SQUAMATA (a.k.a. THE ORAKULOID) is a sleazy pulp surrealist who lives between the scenes. He writes microfictions, hypnopop song lyrics, disquieting confessional comedy essays, graphic novel scripts, dream diaries, and spectral celebutante novels. His work has appeared in *CITY OF WEIRD*, *PropellerMag*, *Hypno Komix*, and *Stealing Time Magazine*. He is currently developing television projects with some associates in the city of screens. You can optically fondle his archives at ORAKULOID.blogspot.com and swim in his spoken word incantations at SoundCloud/jason-squamata. He can be summoned via hypnokomix@gmail.com.

ROBERT TORRES
Robert Torres is a local writer and actor. Their work explores the changeable nature of reality and the trouble of having a body whether you like it or not. They have been featured locally at Á Reading, Salon Skid Row, and elsewhere. They have appeared on stage with Monkey with a Hat on.

JONATHAN VAN BELLE
Jonathan van Belle is a bookseller, book-eater, lover of the love of wisdom, and optimist of a neo-Leibnizian sort. Also, he will pegasize for fish tacos.

GEOFF WALLACE
Geoff Wallace is a 55-year-old trapped in the body of an 18-year-old. His twin selves are at work on many projects at once. He likes shelving picture books at Powell's in Portland, Oregon.

www.ingramcontent.com/pod-product-compliance
Lightning Source LLC
Chambersburg PA
CBHW032021180726
48283CB00008B/2784

9781949127003